MW00902433

Slippers Loves to Run

by **Andrew Clements**
illustrated by **Janie Bynum**

Dutton Children's Books ● New York

For Matthew and Tricia Clements,
whose love for their dogs has brought joy and inspiration to so many
A.C.

To Mo, who loves her puppies!
XO, J.B.

DUTTON CHILDREN'S BOOKS
A division of Penguin Young Readers Group

Published by the Penguin Group

Penguin Group (USA) Inc., 375 Hudson Street, New York, New York 10014, U.S.A.
Penguin Group (Canada), 90 Eglinton Avenue East, Suite 700, Toronto, Ontario, Canada M4P 2Y3
(a division of Pearson Penguin Canada Inc.) • Penguin Books Ltd, 80 Strand, London WC2R 0RL, England
Penguin Ireland, 25 St Stephen's Green, Dublin 2, Ireland (a division of Penguin Books Ltd) • Penguin Group (Australia),
250 Camberwell Road, Camberwell, Victoria 3124, Australia (a division of Pearson Australia Group Pty Ltd)
Penguin Books India Pvt Ltd, 11 Community Centre, Panchsheel Park, New Delhi - 110 017, India • Penguin Group (NZ),
Cnr Airborne and Rosedale Roads, Albany, Auckland 1310, New Zealand (a division of Pearson New Zealand Ltd)
Penguin Books (South Africa) (Pty) Ltd, 24 Sturdee Avenue, Rosebank, Johannesburg 2196, South Africa
Penguin Books Ltd, Registered Offices: 80 Strand, London WC2R 0RL, England

Text copyright © 2006 by Andrew Clements
Illustrations copyright © 2006 by Janie Bynum
All rights reserved.

Clements, Andrew, date.
Slippers loves to run / by Andrew Clements ; illustrated by Janie Bynum.—1st ed.   p. cm.
Summary: Slippers the dog loves to run, as long as Mommy, Daddy, Laura, and Edward are there
to catch and hug him when he slows down.
ISBN 0-525-47648-2 (alk. paper)
1. Dogs—Juvenile fiction. [1. Dogs—Fiction. 2. Family—Fiction. 3. Hugging—Fiction.]
I. Bynum, Janie, ill. II. Title.
PZ10.3.C5937Sln 2006
[E]—dc22   2005029397

Published in the United States by Dutton Children's Books,
a division of Penguin Young Readers Group
345 Hudson Street, New York, New York 10014
www.penguin.com/youngreaders

Designed by Beth Herzog

Manufactured in China   First Edition

1 3 5 7 9 10 8 6 4 2

Slippers has four little paws.
He loves to make them run.

Slippers has four people.

He loves to make them run, too.

In the big backyard Slippers runs and runs and runs.
Slippers can run faster than Laura.
He can run faster than Mommy.
He can run faster than Daddy.

And Slippers can run a LOT faster than Edward.

But Slippers always slows down.
Then Laura says, "I got him!"
Edward says, "Me, too!"

And Edward and Laura give Slippers a big hug.
That's why Slippers loves to run.

One Saturday, Slippers wanted everyone to run with him. He ran around and around Mommy.

But Mommy was planting the flowers.
Mommy said, "Not now, Slippers."

He ran around and around Edward.

But Edward was playing in the sandbox.
Edward said, "No!" and kept digging.

Slippers ran around and around Daddy.

But Daddy was fixing the swings.
Daddy said, "Not now, Slippers."

Slippers ran around and around Laura.

But Laura was helping Daddy.
She said, "Too busy, Slippers."

So Slippers ran alone.
He ran around the swing set.

He ran around the garden.

He ran around the sandbox.

Then Slippers ran all the way around the house.

Slippers stopped running at the front gate.
He tilted his head to listen.

The wind made a sound, and so did the gate.
It went *crreeeaaakk.*

And when it made that sound,
there was an open place.
The open place was as big as a puppy.

Slippers put his nose through
the open place. He sniffed.

It didn't smell like Daddy out there.
It didn't smell like Mommy.
It didn't smell like Laura out there.
And it didn't smell like Edward.
It smelled BIG out there.

Slippers took one step out.
He had two paws out
and two paws in.
Plus one tail.

Slippers took another step out.
Then he had four paws out
and one tail in.

Slippers turned around to see
if his tail would follow him,
and it did.

Slippers looked back into the open place.
He saw the front door of his big house.
He saw his digging place by the bushes.
It looked good in there. Then the gate went
crreeeaaakk—and the open place was gone.

Slippers felt scared.
He started to look for a way to go in.
But then he had an itch.

So Slippers sat down on the sidewalk and
scratched. Then he scratched some more.

When the itch was gone, Slippers stood up.
He put his nose up high and sniffed and
sniffed and sniffed.

Everything smelled so big.
And it all smelled so new.
And something smelled like . . . FOOD!

So Slippers began to run along the sidewalk
all by himself. He ran and ran, sniffing the food.
And when his nose told him to, Slippers turned
and ran between some bushes.

After the bushes there was grass.
A daddy was there. But it wasn't Daddy.
And an edward was there. But it wasn't Edward.

And the food was there, too,
right in front of Slippers.

The edward said, "Here,"
and gave some food to Slippers.

The daddy said, "Hey!"
and he threw his hat at Slippers!

So Slippers dropped the food.
He ran through the bushes,
and he ran along the sidewalk all by himself.

Slippers ran and ran until he came to a big yard.
A mommy was there. But it wasn't Mommy.
And a laura was there. But it wasn't Laura.

She went running after a ball.
So Slippers ran and got the ball first.

Then the laura ran the other way.
The laura said, "Help! Help!" and ran to the mommy.
The mommy shook a stick at Slippers,
and she said, "Shoo! Shoo!"

Slippers dropped the ball and ran away fast.
When he got to the sidewalk, he ran and ran.
He ran so much that his paws began to hurt.
He ran so much that his tongue began to drip.

He ran so much that he had to stop.
Slippers lay down by the sidewalk.
His mouth was open, and the air went inandout
and inandout and inandout and inandout.

Slippers closed his eyes.
Running wasn't fun anymore.

Slippers stopped panting.
He closed his mouth, and then
he sniffed. Slippers opened his eyes
and put up his nose and sniffed again.

Edward! Laura! Mommy! Daddy!

Slippers was home again. He could tell
by the smell. But Slippers was out,
and his people were in. So Slippers put his
front paws on the front gate, and he barked.
And the gate barked back.
It went *crreeeaaakk.*

Slippers saw an open place. It was only as big as a puppy's nose. Slippers put his nose into that open place and pushed.

The open place got bigger and bigger until it was as big as a whole puppy. And the puppy who went running through it was Slippers.

Slippers ran all the way around the house.
Then he ran around and around Daddy
and Mommy and Laura and Edward.
And Laura said "Look! Let's catch Slippers!"

Slippers was tired of running alone.
So he slowed down.

Then Laura said, "I got him!"
Edward said, "And I got him!"
Mommy said, "Me, too!"
And Daddy said, "We've all got him!"

And in the middle of the biggest hug,
Slippers remembered why he loves to run.